This Walker book belongs to:

_____

_____

_____

Poojo's Got Wheels

by Charrow

WALKER BOOKS
AND SUBSIDIARIES
LONDON • BOSTON • SYDNEY • AUCKLAND

This is Poojo.

He was born without back legs.

But he's got wheels.

He can do anything.

He does fancy tricks.

He's got cool pockets to store stuff.

He's a good friend to everyone ...

and everything.

He is fast and clever.

Poojo's got a flat tyre.

Good thing Poojo is also extremely creative.

Too big.

Too small.

Definitely too dangerous.

Aha!

Go, Poojo! Go!

What a good dog you are!

To my mom, who believed in me even when
I couldn't see the way forward

First published 2021 by Walker Books Ltd
87 Vauxhall Walk, London SE11 5HJ

2 4 6 8 10 9 7 5 3 1

© 2021 Charrow

The right of Charrow to be identified as author and illustrator of this work has been asserted by them
in accordance with the Copyright, Designs and Patents Act 1988

This book has been typeset in Sariah

Printed in China

British Library Cataloguing in Publication Data:
a catalogue record for this book is available from the British Library

ISBN 978-1-4063-9987-5

www.walker.co.uk